Dear Parents:

The **Ready Reader Storybooks**™ were created especially for children in kindergarten through second grade. This series is designed to increase children's reading skills and promote their interest in reading by themselves. The stories are enjoyable, with easy-to-follow plot structures and familiar settings. Colorful illustrations help develop young imaginations while adding visual appeal to the reading experience. Young children will be comfortable with the format and the large type.

With a variety of stories to accommodate individual interests, the **Ready Reader Storybooks**™ can help develop basic abilities and encourage your children's independent reading.

Printed in the U.S.A.

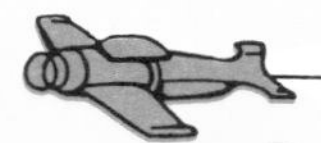

Ready Reader Storybooks™

SAM AND PEPPER'S TREE HOUSE

Written by Eugene Bradley Coco
Illustrated by Linda Blassingame

Modern Publishing
A Division of Unisystems, Inc.
New York, New York 10022

One day, Sam and Pepper went for a walk in the woods.

They saw many trees,
with many branches.

Pepper jumped up on one of the branches.

Sam climbed up to get him.
Then they both sat down
on the branch.

From up high, Sam and Pepper
could see far, far away.

They saw blue lakes,
and green hills.
They even felt close to the clouds.

Sam liked sitting in the tree.
So did Pepper.

Sam had an idea.
She told Pepper.

"Woof! Woof!" Pepper barked.

Sam knew it was a good idea.
They were going to build a tree house.

Sam got the wood.

Pepper fetched the rope.

Pepper got all tied in knots.

Sam laughed.

Pepper laughed, too.

Then Sam got the nails, a hammer, a saw, some paint, and a brush.

NAILS
PAINT

Sam sawed the wood very carefully.
Pepper helped paint the sign—
he didn't need a brush!

SAM and
PEPPER'S
TREE
HOUSE

"Sam and Pepper's Tree House" it read.

Sam nailed in the last board.

"SAM and
PEPPER'S
TREE
HOUSE"

The tree house was done.

Sam and Pepper climbed
into their tree house...

...and smiled.